For
Maddie & Emma
and
Cole & Annabel

2020 Orange County, California

ISBN Numbers 978-0-578-62909-4 (paperback) 978-0-578-62910-0 (hardcover)

Library of Congress Control Number: 2020905161

Our class is a FAMILY

written by
Shannon Olsen

Illustrated by
Sandie Sonke

When you think of a family,
you might picture one in a house:

A mom, a dad, a couple of kids,
plus their dogs and a pet mouse.

Perhaps you think of Grandma

or a stepmom and stepdad.

It could be those 14 cousins

or that twin who makes you mad.

But family doesn't have to be who you're related to.

It can be another special group
who love and care for you.

Have you ever thought about
where most of your time is spent?
It's at school with all of us.
That's where all those hours went!

So if our classroom is the place
where we spend our days,

why wouldn't we want to make it like a home in many ways?

It's a place where we can show respect and kindness to each other, a spot where we can be ourselves and make memories with one another.

We'll have things in common,
these are connections that we'll seek.

But we'll still celebrate our differences
and what makes us each unique.

Our classroom is a special haven where it's okay to make mistakes.

We learn from them and try again,
no matter what it takes.

We'll all have tough days sometimes,
but your teacher is here for you.

And as long as you're a friend to others,
your peers will be there too.

In this classroom of four walls,
we will stick together.

We'll help each other learn and grow in any kind of weather.

So let's always remember
what a great team we can be.
You have our back, and we have
yours. We're a classroom family.

About the Author

Shannon Olsen is a second grade teacher from Southern California, with a Masters in Education from University of California, Irvine. She loves traveling and spending time with her husband Jeff, and her two daughters, Madeline and Emma. Shannon is an elementary education blogger at life-between-summers.com, and enjoys creating resources for teachers to use in their classrooms.

About the Illustrator

Sandie Sonke is also a Southern California native with a degree in studio art from California State University Fullerton. She is a fan of coffee and cooking, and among the many hats she wears, her favorite roles are being a wife and mom of two. Sandie has published several children's books, and you can also find more of her freelance illustration work at www.sandiesonkeillustration.com.

Made in the USA
Coppell, TX
12 August 2020